FEB 03 2016
D0984127

For my family, with thanks for the free-range childhood



Published in Canada and the United States of America by Tundra Books,
a division of Random House of Canada Limited, a Penguin Random House Company

Library of Congress Control Number: 2014951815



Library and Archives Canada Cataloguing in Publication

Wahl, Phoebe, author, illustrator
Sonya's chickens / Phoebe Wahl.

Issued in print and electronic formats.
ISBN 978-1-77049-789-4 (bound).—ISBN 978-1-77049-791-7 (epub)

I. Title.

PZ7.W1337So 2015 j813'.6 C2014-906442-X
C2014-906443-8

Edited by Samantha Swenson
Designed by Andrew Roberts
The artwork in this book was watercolor, collage and colored pencil.
The text was set in Gararond.

www.penguinrandomhouse.ca

Printed and bound in China

1 2 3 4 5 6 20 19 18 17 16 15

# SONYA'S CHICKENS

PHOEBE WAHL

Tundra Books

One day, Sonya's papa came home with three fluffy chicks. He gave the chicks to Sonya.

"It can be your job to take care of them," he told her.

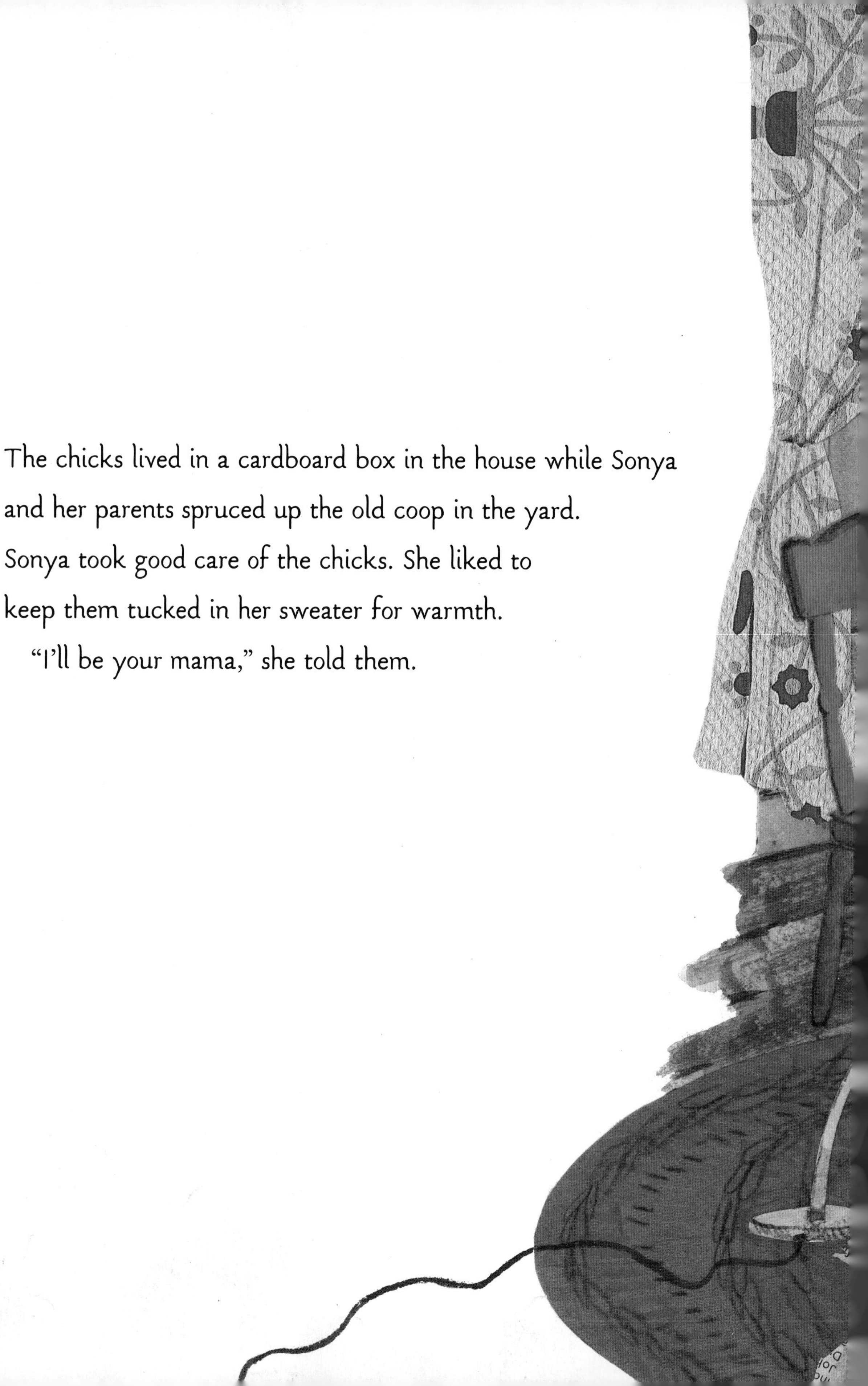

The chicks lived in a cardboard box in the house while Sonya and her parents spruced up the old coop in the yard. Sonya took good care of the chicks. She liked to keep them tucked in her sweater for warmth.

"I'll be your mama," she told them.

here he finds
by a goateed football jock who
English subtitles.) The
of course, the dan-

Sonya took her job of tending to the chickens very seriously, and they grew quickly into gawky pullets. As her mama and papa went about the duties of the farm, Sonya was proud to do her part. Everywhere Sonya went, her little birds were at her heels, peeping loudly.

Every morning, Sonya would rise to the crow of the old rooster and let the chickens out of their coop to forage and play.

Sonya made sure her chickens had enough water. She cleaned their coop and gave them fresh straw.

She fed them by scattering cracked corn on the ground and even let them peck it from her hands. Sometimes, the chickens found worms for their dessert.

In Sonya's care, they were soon healthy full-grown hens.

One morning, Sonya found a smooth, brown egg nestled in one hen's straw bed. She put the soft egg against her cheek and said, "Thank you."

Sonya was a good mama to her chickens.

Every night, Sonya made sure her chickens were tucked safely in their coop. As they cooed and clucked themselves to sleep, Sonya would latch the coop door and carefully shut the gate behind her before heading to her own warm home.

One chilly night,
Sonya woke to a ruckus of squawking
and shuffle-y bump noises from outside. Her heart
beating quickly, she rubbed sleep from her eyes, pulled
on her boots and crept out to check on her birds.
The night sky was big and cold, and Sonya wished
she had woken her papa to keep her safe from
the rustling bushes and shadows.

The floor of the coop was frosted with feathers, and Sonya cried out as she counted not three, but two frightened chickens cowering in the rafters above. The third was nowhere to be seen. Sonya burst into tears. Before she knew it, strong arms scooped her up and she cried into her papa's beard.

Sonya's papa carried her into the house and held her close. When Sonya had exhausted herself with crying, she asked, "What took her? A fox? Did it kill her? It's not FAIR!"

"Shhh," said Sonya's papa. "What might seem unfair to you might make sense to a fox."

And he told her a story.

"The fox who took your chicken lives in the woods beyond the field," Sonya's papa said. "He works hard every day to find food to bring home to his babies. Most of the time he can find mice and moles, but sometimes the fox needs a big meal for his family, so he does everything he can to find one. He didn't know or care that it was our chicken he took. He just saw a chance to feed his family. I know you feel sad, but you wouldn't want those baby foxes to go hungry, would you?"

Sonya thought about it. "No," she said. "I guess not."

"The fox's baby is called a kit, like a baby chicken is a chick and you are a child," said Sonya's papa. "I do everything I can to make sure you are happy, and have a full belly and a warm place to sleep. You did everything *you* could to make sure your chicks were happy and had full bellies and a warm place to sleep. Because you love your chicks like I love you. The fox is no different. He loves his kits too. So even though it's sad for us, we can understand why he did it."

The next morning, Sonya laid a few special stones to mark a grave for her chicken in the corner of the yard. Together, she and her family remembered their hen who had been soft, who had loved worms and who had laid that first smooth, brown egg.

"A bird who was loved," Sonya's mama said, giving her a kiss.

Sonya's heart was heavy. But as she mourned her chicken, she thought too of the happy baby foxes living deep in the woods.

Sonya and her family repaired and reinforced the broken siding of the coop where the fox had gotten in. And while she was still a little sad, Sonya remained vigilant in caring for her other two hens. She made sure they had enough water. She cleaned their coop and gave them fresh straw and scattered cracked corn for them to eat.

Best of all was the day that one of the smooth, brown eggs began to crack.

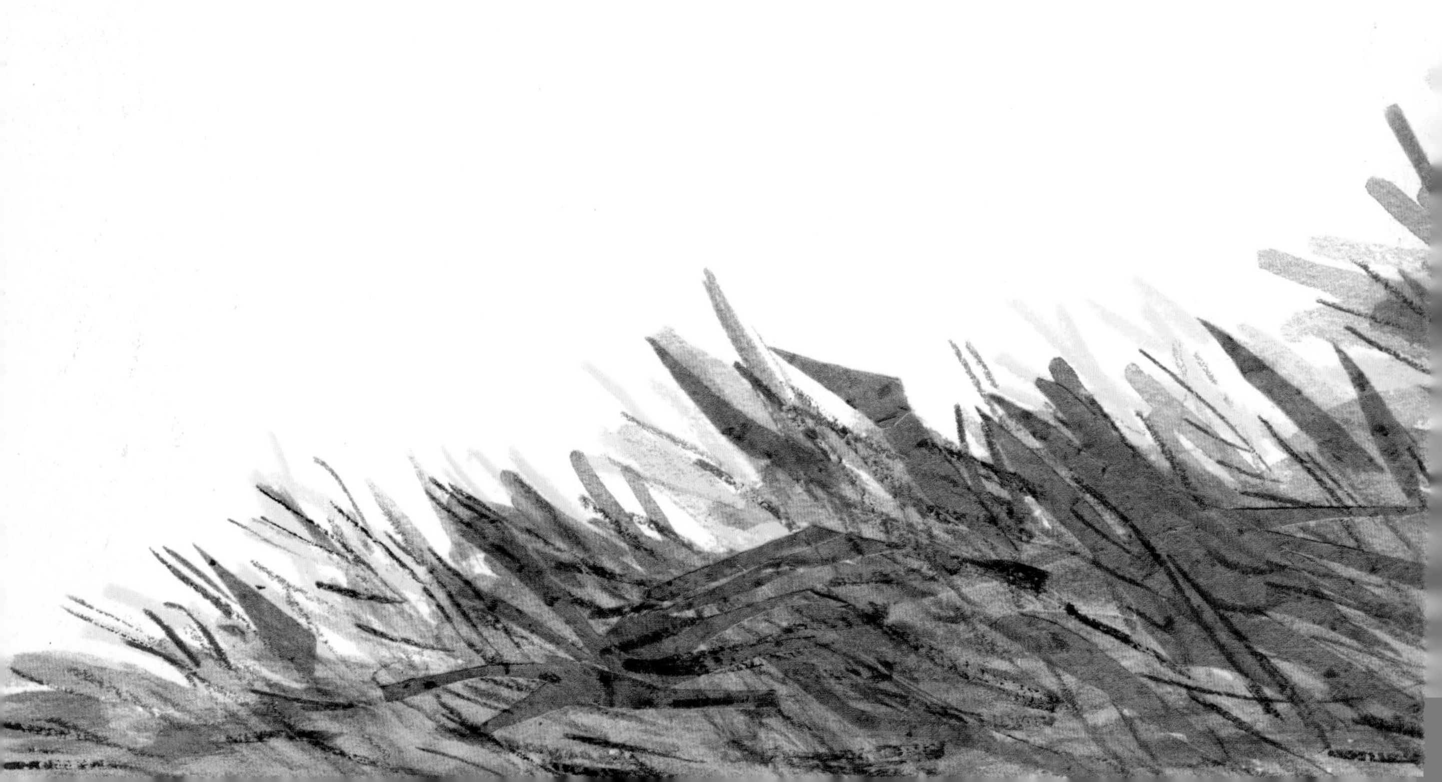

To her delight, Sonya had a brand new chick.
“I will be your mama,” she said. “I will do
everything I can to make sure you are happy and
have a full belly and a warm place to sleep.”
And she did.